D0607283

CATERPILLAR BOOKS

1 The Coda Centre, 189 Munster Road,
London SW6 6AW

First published in Great Britain 2011

Text copyright © Caterpillar Books Ltd 2011

Illustrations copyright ©
Jack Tickle 2005 and 2011

All rights reserved

ISBN: 978-1-84857-254-6

Printed in China

CPB/1800/0203/0612

10 9 8 7 6 5 4 3 2

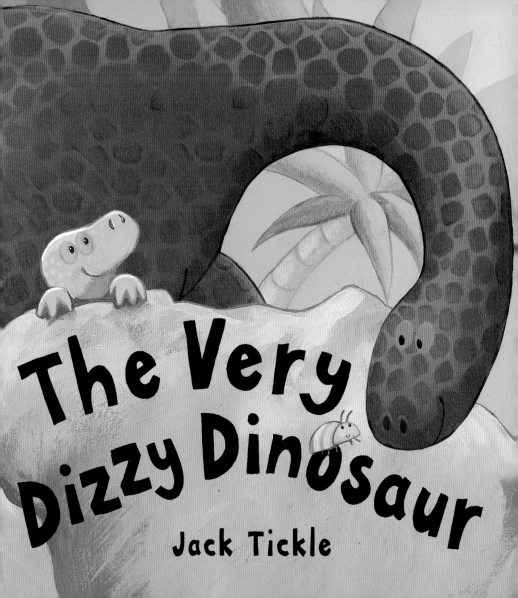

The Very Dizzy Dinosaur

Jack Tickle

I am Stegosaurus,
A dizzy dinosaur.

SWISH!

oOOH!

My friends would like to meet you,
So let's go and explore!

OOOOUCH!

"I'm on my way to eat you up!"
Velociraptor warns.
But look what's stopped him in his tracks –
A prickly patch of thorns!

OOOH!

Ichthyosaurus dips and dives –
He's like a giant fish.

SWISH!

Just watch out for the ripples
When he gives his tail a swish!

Diplodocus stalks the land –
His tail swings to and fro.
All the smaller dinosaurs
Must be careful how they go!

SWISH!

EEK!

THUD!

Triceratops is on the charge –
He's such a scary sight.
But really he's just running scared
Because he's had a fright!

EEK!

Splishy-splashing all about,
This monster of the sea

WHOOSH!

Is called Elasmosaurus
And he's fishing for his tea!

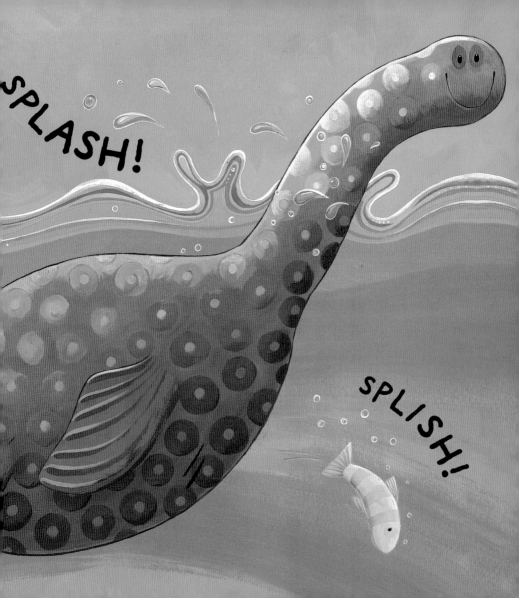

Flapping like a giant bird
Pteranodon is proud –
Her baby chicks are hatching out
To join the dino crowd!

FLAP!

FLAP!

ROAARR!

Now meet Tyrannosaurus –
He likes to show his claws.
Just be sure you're out of sight
When he opens his huge jaws!